The Wasporcist

AMY LAURENS

OTHER WORKS

SANCTUARY SERIES

Where Shadows Rise
Through Roads Between
When Worlds Collide

KADITEOS SERIES

How Not To Acquire A Castle

SHORT STORY COLLECTIONS

Of Sea Foam and Blood
Darkness and Good

NON-FICTION

How To Write Dogs
How To Theme
How To Create Cultures

Find other works by the author at
www.amylaurens.com

The Wasporcist

INKLET #5

AMY LAURENS

www.inkprintpress.com

Print ISBN: 978-1-925825-05-3
eBook ISBN: 9781386387763

www.inkprintpress.com

National Library of Australia Cataloguing-in-Publication Data
Laurens, Amy 1985 –
The Wasporcist
32 p.
ISBN: 978-1-925825-05-3
Inkprint Press, Canberra, Australia
1. Young Adult Fiction—Fantasy 2. Young Adult
Fiction—Short Stories 3. Young Adult Fiction—Horror

First Print Edition: March 2019
Cover design © Inkprint Press
Interior art © Heather Craik

THE WASPORCIST

Today.

MY EARS WON'T STOP RINGING. IT'S been a week now—ever since Halloween, actually. That party was insane. I prob'ly shouldn't have let that guy pour me a drink, even if he did compliment my outfit.

But anyway, the ringing. Every noise echoes in my left ear with a weird, computerized-voice-over effect. It's especially bad in a crowd, since the echoes get so loud I can't understand what anyone is saying.

I went to the doctor today. She says nothing's wrong. I think she thinks I'm making it up.

Nov 8.

Ear ringing persists. It's like the electricity in my brain is going mad, buzzing so loud I can hear it.

Will my brain explode, I wonder?

Day after yesterday.

The buzzing is so loud now I have trouble hearing anything else. At least it means I can't hear things echoing.

First day of the rest of forever, in which I never hear again.

Have determined that my brain has been replaced with a wasp, and it's mad at being trapped in my pitiful skull, hence continuous buzzing. Must see an insectologist, or whatever it is that they're called, to get it out.

Nov 13.

It's Friday. I should have known that was a bad start. Insectologist, who is apparently actually called an entomologist, tells me that wasps don't live in people's heads. I told him I'm always an exception. He told me to call a shrink.

Had shrink. Didn't work. Besides, I don't need a shrink, I need a waspinator. I wonder what they're called. Let me check.

Internet says exterminator. How dull. I vote in favour of waspinator. Let me go call one.

Nov 13, later.

Called. Booked. Didn't tell the guy where the wasp was; just said 'up there' when he asked. Hope he comes prepared.

Another day.

Waspinator should be coming today, wootwoo. I am so SICK of this buzzing. I swear, the thing is driving me insane. Even Josh thinks I'm acting weird, and he'd know, he's the King of Weird.

Oh, knock at the door. That'll be the Waspinator. I'll report back in a minute.

Later.

The guy looked at me like I was mad when I told him the wasp was in my head. "Too right it is," he said. I think that was a little uncalled for. Still, I made him check, just to be sure. He shone a light in through my ear and said he couldn't see anything that wasn't supposed to be there.

Personally, I'm suspicious. I think if I looked in *his* ear I wouldn't see anything at all. Ha. Idiot.

But seriously, what am I going to now? Who am I going to call?

...Who you gonna call? Ghost! Busters! Dun da-dun dun-dun.

HEY! That's actually not a bad idea! What if it's *not* a wasp? What if it's, like, a demon who's just *pretending* to be a wasp?

That's so awesome I'm practically bouncing in my seat. Who do you call for demons, again? Exercise-thingies. What are they called? Oh yeah, exorcists. Right.

snigger Wasporcists. That's what I need: a wasporcist. But I doubt that'll be in the phone book. I supposed I'll just try for a generic exorcist first.

I'll let you know how it goes, diary-m'dear.

Even later.

I love coincidence. Got this mad phone call earlier that Josh took. Sounded like it was one of those sales calls, you know? The ones where they try to sell you a trip to Hawaii or insurance for your fish or something? Yeah. Those. But anyway, I was listening, and so I heard when Josh told the guy that we didn't need an exorcist.

I practically snatched the phone out of his hand, I was so excited. I mean, seriously? What are the odds?! So awesome. So anyway, exorcist—his name is Brad—agreed to come out. Says it sounds like it could be a demon. He gets situations like this all the time, he said.

Hmm. I wonder if there's, like, a conspiracy of demons, all invading people's heads as wasps? I wonder if Josh has heard buzzing lately?

I just ran out into the hall and asked him. He said he hasn't. Bummer. No conspiracy after all. Oh well. I guess I'll just wait for the exorcist.

Nov 20.

Exorcist is coming, exorcist is coming! I'm so excited. I hope he's cute.

He should be here any minute now—oh, look, see? A knock at the door. I wonder if he knew I was writing about him coming, and that's why he knocked now? I wonder if he's been waiting at the door for, like, half an hour, just waiting for me to sit down and start writing so he could knock just as I wrote about—

I'm COMING, Josh. Sheesh. Let a person finish their sentence, will ya?

Urgh, better go before he comes in here and see this. No one's supposed to know I'm keeping a journal. I'm only doing it 'cause the shrink last year said I should. Not that I ever have anything interesting to write about.

Well, until the whole wasp-invading-my-brain thing.

Bloody hell, Josh, COMING. Right. See me go...

Tonight.

OHMIGOSH! The Wasporcist is totally that guy from the party, you know, the random one who poured me a drink? And he's CUTE.

But yeah, ha, I told you it was a wasp-demon.

Brad took one look and agreed. Said it was a pretty potent demon, though, so he'd have to come back a couple of times and have at it in bits—too strong to tackle all at once. Good thing I sold the car, exorcists aren't cheap.

Mind you, why would they be? With the work *they* have to do? No, thanks.

Makes me shudder. I'm more than happy to pay someone else to do the dirty work. Especially if it means this infernal buzzing will stop.

Dec 2.

Sorry I haven't written in ages, diary-dearest. I've been... occupied. Don't tell Josh, but I think Brad—he's the exorcist I wrote about last time, remember?—I think he has a crush on me. He's come over every single day this week, usually while Josh's at work. He brought me flowers, yesterday. Daisies. My favourite, not that anyone but you knows that.

Josh says he's creepy.

I dunno. He's pretty cute. And I think the buzzing isn't as bad when he's around.

scowl Josh still thinks I'm making it all up. Idiot. I bet he wouldn't even know what *colours* I like.

(Green and purple, for the record.) Anyway. Bed.

Dec 3.

I don't have long, I'm going out to dinner in a minute with—oh, better not say, just in case. I'm sure you can guess. We arranged it this morning when he came over. And guess what he brought with him? Earrings, purple and green ones. He's only known me for two weeks and already he knows more about me than stupid Josh.

Dec 6.

Brad is right. Josh is a dickhead. He's been totally unsympathetic about this whole wasp-demon head-invasion thing, and keeps on ragging at me for the money missing from our bank account. It's not like it's *that* much; Brad is charging me less than half price, since the demon's proving so hard to get rid of. And he told me at dinner the other night that he's barely had *any* clients this month, and he had to negotiate with his landlord to pay double rent for December because he couldn't afford to cover November.

...Maybe I *should* run away. I don't mind being poor. And I know what it's like to be so lonely...

But where can we go?

December nine, three nineteen pm. The moment of my momentous decision.

I'm doing it. Tonight. I'm going to sneak out of the house and I'll meet Brad and he'll take me away from here, away from all of this nonsense. The healing is almost complete, and he'll take me away, and then I'll be totally fixed, and he'll never be lonely again, and everything will be wonderful.

It's not like Josh will even care; he's barely spoken to me since he found me sitting in the corner the other day doodling hearts around Brad's name.

Okay, so that was a tactical mistake, but seriously, if he wasn't such a jerk I wouldn't be thinking of leaving.

No, not thinking, I *am* leaving. Tonight.

Oh, gosh, it gives me shivers just thinking about it. I'm so excited I can hardly wait! I wonder if Brad will mind if I'm early?

I'm going to go pack now, just in case. Can't wait can't wait can't WAIT!!!!

〜〜〜

Josh closed the document, throat burning, chest tight. "Yes," he told the police officer standing behind him. "That's her diary."

"Well, you won't mind if we take the laptop up to the station as evidence then?"

Josh shook his head. What difference did it make?

The officer gave him a sympathetic look. "I'm truly sorry. But your help—well, it might just make the difference between finding the killer and not."

Josh nodded. Sure. Let them think he was a hero, if that's what they wanted. He knew the truth. He'd lost her long before some psycho had torn her body apart in the woods behind the house, and even long before she'd gotten that stupid idea about the wasp in her head.

The psychiatrist had warned him she might never come back. He'd been stupid to hope. And now his ears wouldn't stop ringing.

Honestly, I never realised this story would be as popular as it has been. It was just a quick, off the cuff thing—though later I added in the comment at the beginning about Brad pouring her a drink, to clarify the ending: that Brad is a creepy, predatory, serial-killery *thing*, implanting buzzing *somethings* in people's minds.

Still. It's the short story that is apparently most memorable of mine, to date? So there you go.

What's also interesting about this one, looking back on it, is that although on the surface it clearly belongs to my (accidental) era of punishing stupidity or vapidity with death in stories (reflecting, I think, the fact that I was pretty unforgiving of myself in my twenties), when you consider the ending, it kind of subverts that. Josh hasn't really done anything *wrong*; he's set up to be a nice, relatively caring kind of person, if totally ineffectual at supporting our poor Main Character. But he means well, and unlike Main Character, doesn't display any overt stupidity or vapidity or naivety.

And yet, it's (hopefully) clear from the ending line that now he too has been implanted with this probably supernatural wasp, implying that he is the next target for the killer.

He did nothing wrong, but he's probably going to die anyway.

So although, on the surface, I always felt this was another one of those stories where I had trouble forgiving my own historical naivety, perhaps actually my subconscious knew better all along. She does rather tend to be the more insightful part of my brain.

DOWNLOAD YOUR FREE EBOOK

When you buy a print book from Inkprint Press, we like to say THANK YOU by offering you the ebook for free!

Please head to
www.inkprintpress.com/inklets/5/
and the use the coupon INKLET5 to get your copy of this Inklet in epub AND mobi today!
(Coupon will only work once.)

Read more by this author!

OF SEA FOAM AND BLOOD: TO DUST

Sometimes running away is the hardest thing you can do. What I want, what I really want, is to turn around right now and plunge back into the midst of the Maliche, let their rotting, stinking bodies surround me, and kill as many as I can before I die. For Mum. For Dad. For Joss.

God, please let Joss get away. Mum and Dad might be gone, but please, please… save him. I left him climbing for a rooftop, and the Maliche can't climb, and he might be safe enough—but I have to run, and running is so, so hard when all you want to do is die.

I can't die though, not today. Today I have to live, because in my backpack, weighing me down like guilt, is the box. It's a perfect cube I can balance on one hand, sharp-edged and shined to perfection—a magic box, the only hope we have of stopping the Maliche forever. And I want to stop them more than anything else in the world, more than I want to die, because while there are Maliche, no one dies.

And so I run, heading north in a town that runs south towards the battle, running for life and death and salvation along a road whipped by the wind and smogged with dust.

From dust created, to dust returned. Only that's exactly it: with the Maliche on our doorstep, there is no return. I've seen the bodies they leave behind, twisted, gruesome things with flesh squeezed until the insides pop, left in the sun to ferment with a rictus of pain on their faces.

And the eyes. The eyes are the worst.

No. Running away is hard, but it must be done. Humanity needs to die.

Keep reading! Head to
http://www.amylaurens.com/books/short-stories/of-sea-foam-and-blood/
to buy your copy now!

AMY LAURENS is an Australian author of fantasy fiction for all ages. She's not actually particularly scared of wasps, but her subconscious is terrified of spiders: they are her only recurring nightmare, despite the fact that in her waking life, she's usually the first to relocate them to outside.

Amy has written a middle grade fantasy trilogy (the *Sanctuary* series), and this year (2019) her comedic fantasy trilogy is coming out, starting with *How Not To Acquire A Castle*.

You can find out more about Amy at her website, www.amylaurens.com.

INKLETS

Collect them all! Released on the 1st and 15th of each month.

SEVENTY
LIANA BROOKS

A Final Request
for Mercy
AMY LAURENS

the kitten psychologist
vs.
the kitten's owners
THEA VAN DIEPEN

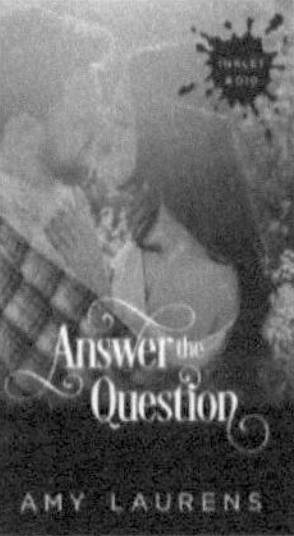

Answer the
Question
AMY LAURENS

Happily,
Red
AMY LAURENS

the kitten psychologist
tries to be patient
through email
THEA VAN DIEPEN

DRAGON
Tuesday
AMY LAURENS

RED PLANET
REFUGEES
LIANA BROOKS

the kitten psychologist &
What The Kitten Did
THEA VAN DIEPEN

Cherry Blossom
AMY LAURENS

Alone
AMY LAURENS

the kitten psychologist
& The Kitten
Come To A Conclusion
THEA VAN DIEPEN

LEVEL NINE
LIANA BROOKS

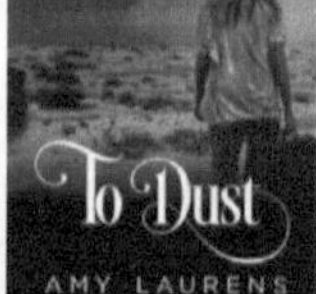
To Dust
AMY LAURENS

Interchange
AMY LAURENS

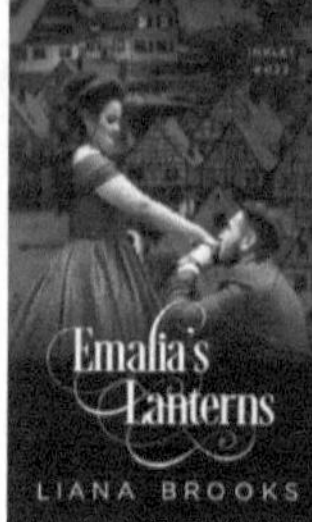
Emalia's
Lanterns
LIANA BROOKS

Dear Santa
AMY LAURENS

The
Quilt-Maker's
Scrap
AMY LAURENS